Other Books By: Anthony Norton

PeeWee I Swear I'm Not Lying
Life Is Untittled
The Measurements Of Outdoors

All Books Are Avaible Now On Amazon!

Soical Media:
Instagram: @antnorton
Twitter: @Norton_ant1

# Our Community

By: Anthony Norton

# Dedication

This book is dedicated to urban communities across the world, where everyone knows everyone and everyone face the same struggles.

In these communities across America, African Americans have been dealing with adversity since the beginning of time. Not being accepted never bothered us, because since the beginning of time we have always fought only to receive the smallest pieces of the pie.

As a brilliant creator, I did my best to share stories of what goes on in urban communities without my characters hearing a response. This book is personalized for the reader to formulate their own opinion on each scenario. I hope you guys enjoy this project that I worked extremely hard on.

Thank you!

# A Firm Believer
By: The Community
(The Survivors)

I am great, I am blessed, I am who I am and who I'm supposed to be. I will not let my environment hold me back from my destination and I will fight through my hardest times even when I feel like giving up. I will rely on God's word and wisdom for decisions that I am not certified to make. I will not fear anything on the other side of the door and I will strive to be great because it was destined for me. I am great, I am blessed, I am who I am and who I'm supposed to be.

## Young & Unaware
### By: William Williamson
### (Community Mentor)

This is strictly for the youth, with y'all selfish, ungrateful asses. Now, I'm not referring to the children who can't control the environment they are raised in, I am mainly talking to the teenagers and young adults who know better. Understand that I'm not trying to be disrespectful or embarrass you guys, I'm just very aggravated and troubled with the way y'all are carrying on in society. I get sick to my stomach when I see young males on social media posing with guns in one hand and drugs in the other.

Are you aware of the violent persona you are creating within yourself? Sooner or later, posing for a pic (picture) won't be enough, and you will feel the need to use that gun for some foolishness. And to my little sister's, it bothers me to see y'all display your body parts for a like, comment, or a dm (direct message) from somebody that cares less about loving you the right way. I just want y'all to hear me out before y'all think I'm trying to belittle what y'all think is cool. Like the great rapper J. Cole once said "I'm stuck in the middle of two generation I'm little bro and big bro all at once." With that being said I feel like it's my responsibility to be "big bro" to the younger generation, hopefully I can inspire you all to use this precious life for something positive rather than validation.

Young & Unaware Part 2
By: William Williamson
(Community Mentor)

This disturbs me. This is a parenting problem that has turned into a community problem. We are failing our kids. If you're not a part of the solution, you're a part of the problem.

— William Williamson

Just the other day on social media, I watched a 13 year old boy smoke weed with a 380 pistol tucked into his pants. As he spoke live on Facebook, he goes on a rant to say: "I stay lit (meaning high off drugs) all I do is smoke the best drugs. If you need that real shit holla at me or just follow me on the gram (meaning Instagram). I'm telling y'all, y'all missing out. And for all y'all haters… I keep that 380 on me." And he lifted up his shirt to show off the black pistol. I watched all 3 minutes and 13 seconds of the video and I scrolled down to notice over 2 thousand views, nine hundred likes, and the video had been shared over five hundred times, a viral video I would say. Right then, that's when it struck me. It's not the youths fault for their disruptive behavior in society, we the adults are to blame. The mothers, fathers, older brothers, sisters and they wanna be mentors. We are the blame for our youth carrying so much hate and violence in their hearts. For once, we have to stop blaming them for what they have been taught from our actions. A baby isn't born talking, they must go through the learning stages and that's the same with our

3

teenagers.

They are not learning this toxic behavior on their own. It's being showcased to them and being passed down from generation to generation. So, when you see the youth carry on in such an outrageous way just know it's a learned behavior and we can't blame them. We have to blame ourselves and change ourselves and that's how we will change the youth that will lead our culture someday.

A Man After God's Heart
By: Brother Nelson
(God millennium disciple)

"Good morning Church."
"Good morning brother Nelson." The church replied. "I won't stand up here too long, I don't want to be holding service up. I figured since we are all giving our testimony and thanking God for his never ending grace, that I should share the blessings he has rained upon me. Brother Nelson adjusted the microphone and took a deep breath. "First off, Can I get an Amen?" Brother Nelson said, wiping the sweat from his face with his handkerchief. "I want to give thanks to Jesus Christ who is in control of my life. Second, I want to thank God for his everlasting love and his divine grace he shows to me and my beautiful family. My son Bryson, my daughter Aaliyah and tremendous wife Elaina who is the backbone of this family. I couldn't ask for a better family than the one I have. Three years ago around this time, I was jobless, my wife and I had some deep rooted issues in our marriage and the kids weren't doing well in school. But, God turned all that around after I gave all my troubles to him. I remember it like it was yesterday. While my wife was at work and the kids were in school, I fell to my knees at the edge of my bed and cried out in prayer. I mean, I prayed myself to sleep. I told God that I was turning all my problems over to him and that he will take care of them because it was written in the Bible for me to cast my sins upon him. And church, I tell you, ever

since that day, God has been with me. I have found a job, the wife and I have stopped arguing and both of my kids are straight "A" students. I praise God for his everlasting love. He is the reason that I can stand here and say, Jesus is real and he's coming back for his people.

## Ghetto fabulous
### By: Shaniqua Blackmon
### (The daughter of Kimberly)

Oh Lord, if this white woman calls mama ghetto one more time under her breath, Publix employees are gonna have to help her off the floor. Because mama is gonna slap the racism out of her mouth. Does she not know you can't just go around calling black women anything other than their name? She really had the audacity to call mama ghetto, because she's using food stamps for our groceries. She's lucky mama hasn't dragged her pale white ass across the floor by her blonde hair. Although, mama didn't address the lady yet, I could just tell mama was aggravated by her huffing and puffing, because mama had started to pace her body weight from one side to the other while clutching onto her keychain that was strapped to her purse with a small can of mace. I covered my eyes with my hands while holding my glitter lip gloss from the hair store. Mama turned around and opened her mouth to address the lady and all I could think was "great another store we're getting banned from because mama got into a fight." To my surprise, mama turned around and said, "Ma,am with all due respect, I would appreciate it if you didn't use that language in front of my daughter. If anyone is ghetto in here, that would be you. I don't understand how you can be so comfortable to name call someone you don't even know. And for the record, not everyone that receives help from the government is from the ghetto. Because if I can be honest, I've never spent a night living in the slums. Yeah, my community maybe ran down and a little beat up but I will never reference it as the ghetto. Learn a person's story before you say such a thing. I lost my job months ago. My daughter needed me home because leukemia nearly took her life. As you can see God has blessed her, and the devil in you is trying to tear his blessed one's down, but it's not going to happen today. So you have a nice day

Ms. "I AM TOO IMPATIENT." Mama grabbed the groceries from the cashier and ordered me to come. Even though Mama stormed out pissed, I stormed out feeling proud, happy and excited. I was proud of the way mama handled the situation by expressing herself with words and not violence like I have seen in the past. I was happy to see my beautiful, hard working mother who I look up to stand up for herself like she tells me to do all the time. I couldn't be more excited to see mama change like she promised she would.

## City Hall
## By: Betty-Ann
## (The community mother)

Today I have plans. Plans to demand a meeting with the city mayor, because he's not returning my calls. Although my finances place me in poverty, I pay my damn taxes just like everyone else. So I will be demanding a meeting, and I have questions that need answers. He has to explain to me why the light at the corner of my street still hasn't been fixed, he has to explain why there are still pot holes in the middle of MLK boulevard and he better come up with a good reason why there's no activity center after so many kids have been hit by a car or shot in the park. I don't understand how the people keep voting him in. There should be some kind of law to stop him from running for office. But since there's not, his name appears on the ballot, the people keep voting him in office and he keeps stealing the government funds. It surprises me that he showcases such behavior like this. I expect this from other people, but Mayor Vereen was born in the city of Belle Glade. I watched him grow from a rugrat into a fully grown man. His mother and I still play bingo over at the elders club, next to the seafood restaurant. That mother of his sees no wrong in that child. I should expect that because I caught her plenty of times cheating in bingo. That lady will swipe your card right from underneath your eyes. I guess it's true when people say, 'The apple doesn't fall too far from the tree.' However, all of that's changes today; I am tired of our community suffering and being taken advantage of. We as the people don't need empty promises, we need some action. We want to live comfortably just like those folks across the bridge.

Tears of Joy
By: Shaniqua Blackmon
(The smartest fifth grader)


My fifth grade graduation was the time I found out that tears are not always caused by pain. Sometimes people shed tears of joy, excitement, and relief like my mama Kimberly. When my principal called my name to walk across the cafeteria stage, I looked out into the crowd of friends and family and noticed my mama clapping and crying.

I was immediately disturbed. I was worried that she had received another eviction notice or got her car repoed for the fourth time this year. Maybe my dad was still trying to get custody of me for her leaving me in the house alone while she worked an 8 hour graveyard shift. I couldn't enjoy my last day of elementary school, because I was worrying about what situation my mother and I had to face this time. Finally, our graduation ceremony had ended. I immediately ran towards mama for the bad news. We hugged and she kissed me on my cheek while picking lint from my eye lashes.

"Why the tears mom?" I asked. "No reason baby." She said, while patting her cheeks dry with a napkin to clean the smudged make-up. "After all we have been through since your daddy left us, this is the one thing that brought real joy in my life. Look at you baby, just last year around this time you were battling leukemia. Now you're this beautiful healthy young girl, God has rained down his blessings upon you baby. I know I'm not the best mother all the time, but I love you and I would do anything for you."

Mama hugged me and more tears poured out destroying the last bit of make-up she had on her face. I was at a loss for words. Because usually I'm the one that's crying, but this time it's mama. Without thinking I did what she normally does to me when I'm in tears. I hugged her and told her everything was going to be alright as long as we put our trust in God.

## Social Media
### By: Darrell Woodson & Tyler Higgins
### (High school athletes)

What's on your mind?

Status:

**Darrell Woodson:**  If you have an issue with the players that will take a knee before today's games, and still have no idea why they are doing it.
Then please by all means...Unfriend me now! There's no way you don't see what is going on in America and have zero understanding of why the players are not standing for the national anthem. (Posted at 12:30pm)

#UnfriendMeNow#BLM

50 likes 4 comments 1 share

**Tyler Higgins:** Since when can people who have different opinions not be friends?

#EntitledToMyOwnOpinion

**Darrell Woodson:** @Tyler Higgins Because the lack of empathy for people and understanding of those who are complaining about being oppressed and treated as animals within the confines of their own country, would make it less about opinion and more about lacking care... How can we be friends if you don't care about my well-being but I care about yours?

#LackOfCare

**Tyler Higgins:** @Darrell Woodson Well I care about your well-being as much as anyone's, I understand the movement and the views the black community has to the best of my ability being a white man. Personally, I just disagree with the looting and destroying during the protest and I feel like kneeling during the national anthem is not the correct way to do it because the national anthem is about respecting all the soldiers who have given their life for the freedom that both you and I get to enjoy.

I'm not trying to say who's right or wrong, but I am saying the soldiers that gave their life for this country should be respected by all races that have their two foot on American soil.

#RespectOurSoilders

**Darrell Woodson:** @Tyler Higgins First off, let's not make this about our soldiers that serve this country because it's not about them.

But since we are talking about our Brave American soldiers I must say. If kneeling is wrong, protesting gets you beat up or pepper sprayed or shot... when there are veterans who have expressed that they fought for all Americans rights to the freedom that we have today which includes protest...

There were black soldiers who fought in wars like my father and came home to not open arms but open RACISM and KLAN attacks... for you to say protesting during the national anthem is improper is more disrespectful to the soldiers who fought and died in wars for those freedoms and then you are protesting it. But, hey that's just my opinion against yours.

#MyOpinion

**Tyler Higgins:** @Darrell Woodson Not sure if correct. But, like I said in my opinion. I think that all players should stand for the national anthem and show some damn respect to our soldiers that gave their life for this freaking country MAN!

**Darrell Woodson:** @Tyler Higgins Okay Tyler, because I see that you will turn a blind eye to the Police Brutality and Racism that African Americans are facing in this country. Those football players that are kneeling, are kneeling for people like me.

Regular people that don't have a platform to be heard, so I stand behind them just like you stand behind the national anthem that is so important that it means more than human life. I don't blame you for your lack of knowledge, but I do blame you for not wanting to be educated on systemic issues that African Americans are facing in this country for over 400 years and still counting.

And like I said if you have an issue with the players kneeling respectfully before the national anthem and don't know or care to know please by all means...Unfriend me now!

#IDon'tCareWhatYouSay
#RacismComeFromTheDevil
#EducateYourSelf
#BLM
#UnfriendMeNow
#NotAllPeopleAreRaces
#LackOfKnowledge
#BlackPower

I saw what I saw
By: Betty-Ann & Carla
(The community elders)

**Betty-Ann:** I'm 87 years old and I watched the whole thing. During the entire altercation I didn't blink not one time. No need to feel sorry for me, because I'm not the one lying dead on the pavement. Besides, this is not my first time seeing an African American get murder by the hands of the police, and if I live to see 88 it sure won't be the last. It was a brutal intentional death I witnessed. If I had one of those, what would you call it? Alphabet phones or Iphones, whatever the kids call them nowadays. I would have recorded It, and let you judge how quickly the officer pulled his gun. That Poor kid, my heart goes out to his young soul. He was only 14 years old with a bright future ahead of him. But what really ripped my heart is how the other officers stood there and did nothing to help the situation. And when the new reporters come, they're not going to make it any better. They're gonna find ways to dominis the young teen character. If you are going to report something, report facts not lies. But hey, I understand a lie is more entertaining than the truth. I just hope his mother can find the strength to live on because looking for justice is something the government doesn't give.

**Carla:** That poor officer, I just know he was scared for his life. My heart is ruefully broken, watching that young menace attack that harmless officer who happened to be doing a routine stop, which is normal in his case. Before the officer could ask for I.D the teen jumped on him so quickly that my eyes couldn't believe what I was seeing. The news is always reporting about these things happening, but I never thought I'd witness it. During my 70 years on this earth, I never saw a police officer get disrespectful or racially profile anyone. But I can say, I have seen many African Americans disrespect the law with name calling, attacking them and attempts to murder them. Yeah, "THEY" like to call the boys in blue a violent gang. But what about the Black Lives Matter? "THEY" don't think wearing all black looting and rioting is not gang related? That officer did right by shooting that thug because if not that thug was gonna kill him. I just hope that, that officer's family finds the strength daily to support him for what he does for his community, because serving this country isn't easy.

Say "No" to drugs
By: Darrell Woodson
(The High School baseball star)

Crack Cocaine 1984-91, the drug that killed my mother's best friend Shawn, my Uncle Willie T, and David Ruffin from The Temptations. Three important people in my mother's life. My mother told me many stories on how drugs were taking over the south by storm. She saw some of the best athletes, turn into junkies. Me being an athlete, she made me promise that I wouldn't go near cocaine. In fact she made me promise that I wouldn't go within a 10 foot radius of any drug. I promised her she would never have to worry. Whether I make it in major league baseball or not, it's my responsibility to give her comfort and make sure she understands how I feel about drugs. I explained to her that no drug can make me feel good about myself, give me confidence, make me unstoppable, or relax my state of mind. My God above who created the heavens and earth does those things for me. He gives me confidence, power, and has blessed me beyond my wildest dreams. He's the reason for my full ride to the University of Florida and several other division one Universities. He's the reason for all my happiness and I won't dare replace him with any substance.

White Supremacy
By: Teresa (B.J Older sister)
(Careless)

Dear white people,

You and your kids do not own the playground at the park
alone. Stop that white supremacy shit, because you will get
Malcolm X instead of a "Dr. King" if my son ever experiences
mistreatment like this again.

My son was playing on the monkey bars when this white
kid; excuse my writing. I mean, this Caucasian kid expected
my seven year old son to jump down and move because he
wanted to climb the monkey bars.

That's not the part that made me furious; his mother had
the nerve to ask my son to move because her son, who looked
about ten, wanted to climb the monkey bars. Although she
asked my son politely, I'm smart enough to know she asked
in a way insinuating that her son had more privilege to play on
the monkey bars over my son.

She might have thought he was at the playground alone
and he was defenseless, but guess what Karen? He has a father
to defend him. A father that is in his life, lives in the house
with him, and is willing to go beyond measures for him. So I
politely walked over and said, "Excuse me ma'am, my son is
climbing those monkey bars and it would be nice if you tell

your son to wait until my son is done. Thank you!"

Of course she didn't like it, but I didn't care. I felt that it was my business to take a stand for my son. As soon as she left the park, I called my son over and explained to him that he's not second to anyone, and he is equal to everyone in this world.

Ambition
By: Julian Baker
(The smartest kid in the community)

Today history has been made, this calls for a celebration. All those energy drinks late night, and painful meetings with the guidance counselor really paid off. When my friends wanted to go left, I decided to go right and explore the deepest wonders of my unknown. Books that I didn't want to read... I read them. Research papers I didn't care to write... I wrote them and it all paid off. All those tutoring sessions that my mom took out loans for, did not go in vain. I can't wait to get home and let mom know that her son not only got accepted into the top four Ivy League schools, but also received full ride scholarships for all four years. I keep fighting for greatness regardless of my circumstances and I know the sky's the limit for me. Growing up in poverty, your peers try to tell you what's possible for you to accomplish. Some people just lack ambition, and I understand because our environment is depressing but you have to fight. I never gave up, I never stopped fighting and I went after what my heart desired. Now look at me, I get to sit at my kitchen table with my mother and all my loved ones and make a decision on where I'll be going to further my education in Technology.

Make It Make Sense
By: BJ
(The clueless)

I wasn't there when Hoggy (my Cousin Jay murk's friend) was fighting Craig (a dude from cross town). But I heard about Craig getting his ass knocked out. Shaniqua, who is my Cousin Bernice's friend, told me all about it. She said Hoggy hit Craig so hard that tweety bird was circling around his head and a lump the size of a lemon was right above his left eye. I asked what caused them to fight because I never knew they had beef (tension). Shaniqua looked at me clueless before sharing why she thought they were fighting. I could tell she didn't know the real reason because she kept saying: "It was all about respect; one was looking at the other, and the other felt disrespected so something had to be done." I gave Shaniqua a puzzled look, she couldn't be serious. "I understand when you have a problem with a person you solve it. But we're fighting over looks now?" I asked. "That's crazy, seems like a meaningless fight to me.

Hospital Visit
By: B.J
(The young reckless by association)

It's 2:00 o'clock in the morning and we're here at the hospital, because my cousin Jay Murk just got shot. I didn't cry or expected him to die, because this wasn't his first time. He was shot at Goodwin liquor store, the Trap House Booty Club, and uptown where he and his homies hangout.

So when Auntie Jennifer called my mom with the news to hurry down to the hospital, I didn't sweat it because I knew he would pull through. I was expecting my favorite cousin to roll out of those double doors in a wheelchair at any moment. But that wasn't the case this time, instead of his charming smile coming through the doors, it was a Doctor covered in blood approaching our family.

"I'm Sorry Ms. Molares but your son Jaylen did not make it. We did all we could, because he lost so much blood, there was nothing we could do to save him." My aunt Jennifer fell to the floor and started weeping loudly. I looked over at my mama, sister, my cousin Bernice (Jay Murk's sister), and his girlfriend Kiana. They all were crying in silence, while I just stood next to the Fire extinguisher with my mouth opened in shock.

I wasn't sure what to do or what was next, because Jay Murk took care of all of us. Whether it was giving the last of his drug money or protecting us from danger, he was always there. Now that he's gone, I'm confused on what to do. Seeing my family broken by his death, made me think that I needed to step up. I was unsure of what to do, but I knew I had an important decision to make. As much as I wanted to make that decision on my own, I knew that I couldn't. I needed help; I needed someone who was more powerful and sure of the right decision. So I did like my grandfather always told me to "go to God before making a decision." I leaned up against the wall near the emergency exit door and said a silent prayer.

Dear Lord,

I'm not sure where to start but my mind is leading me into trouble. I have this situation that I'm sure you're aware of because you're God and I need help making the right decision about it. Jay Murk was my favorite cousin and now he's with you Lord. I'm in fear that our family will fall apart, so what do I do to prevent that from happening?

I never got a quicker response from God on any prayer until today. My conscience spoke clearly to me. I could pick up where Jay Murk left off and end up like he did or I can finish high school, and be well on my way to a brighter future. That option made more sense to me. Who knows, maybe I will end up with a college degree and a job with a high paying salary. I had to at least give myself the opportunity to win at this game called life.

Discipline
By: Harry Pete
(Darrell thug life friend)

"Fool Low, Fool Low, Fool Low! Maannn! When I tell you, Fool Low was the spot to be last night. I'm talking wall to wall jam packed full of teenagers slowly grinding on each other, bouncing around, throwing chairs at each other and completely acting a fool. Man, we had a blast Darrell, your girl Keira was there too. She asked why you didn't come; I told her you're staying focused on making it to the major league." Harry said while smoking a blunt out in the open.

"That's right homie." Darrell said shoving Harry with a friendly push. "I'm gonna be the next Ken Griffin Jr knocking the ball 300 plus feet over the fence. I'm trying to be the youngest professional baseball player to hit over 20 home runs in my first 50 games. I'm trying to be the Tom Brady of baseball." Darrell added on while pretending to swing a bat.

Harry laughed and said, "believe it or not I believe in you nigga. There's just something about you that makes me believe a hundred percent in your skills. Every time we link up to chill or hangout, baseball is all you ever talk about. I can see you taking over the baseball world and knocking shit out the park just like Hank Aaron."

Harry wasn't lying either, he really did believe in Darrell. Anyone could tell from the way he protected him and made sure he worked on his batting swing everyday. Although Harry quit school, he was good at sports just like Darrell and made sure he didn't fall through the cracks like him. He

26

took Darrell under his wing, and made sure he didn't miss a day from school or practice. If a professional baseball player is what Darrell wanted to be, Harry was going to make his dream a reality by pushing Darrell past his limits.

Friday Nights
By: Mr. Earl Roosevelt
(A City Employee)

"Diana!!!" Earl yelled as he busted through the living room front door. "Can you soft iron my linen suit, I'm going out tonight to hang with the fellas (Earl clapped his hands and danced like James Brown). I just got paid today, I'm gonna head over to Goodwin liquor store and buy me a bottle of that good ol whiskey, because I'm off all weekend and Monday is a holiday. (Claps hands and dances like James Brown again). "Which suit Earl?" Diana yelled from the back room. "The powder ash black one with the short sleeves that goes with my shiny gator skin Stacy Adams. If you look towards the back of the closet you'll see it hanging up with the clear plastic cleaner's bag on it." Earl yelled from the shower.

Moments after Earls shower

"Yeaaahhh!!! (Claps and dance like James Brown for the third time). Yep! That's the suit I was talking about. The classic powder black that goes with my shiny gators Stacy Adam's shoes. Thanks baby! I already cashed my check and put it on the counter down stairs in the kitchen. I took $20 out for my whiskey. So take the rest for the payment of the bills and go shopping for yourself." Earl said while racing to get dressed.

"So where are you hanging out tonight?" Diana said

with her hand on her hips. "I'm just going down the street to Willie Jones house to play some domino's and get drunk. I'll be home before 12 midnight." Earl said while combining his Afro towards the back. After he was done he kissed Diana on the lips and ran out the front door singing Sir Charles song 'It's Friday.'

Workforce/More Life
By: Julian Baker
(The young entrepreneur)
(Summer Job)

As I operate this pallet jack offloading a semi-truck trailer, I think to myself "I can't do this forever." It hurts to think that waking up at four in the mornings of every Monday, Thru, Friday, and even sometimes Saturday could be a part of my life forever. I know; "If a man doesn't work, a man shouldn't eat." But a man who works as hard as I do should be eating steak instead of a short stack of Pringles.

I mean fifteen dollars an hour sounds good, but after tax deductions you're left with just enough to pay your bills (and maybe a tall stack of Pringles). And no I'm not talking about the extra bills that are created, I'm talking about bills that you can't live without like; rent or a mortgage, lights, water and although some may not look at health insurance as a bill, that too still has to be paid.

I don't understand why I have to work 40 hours a week just to receive a check that's going towards bills. Help me to understand that. You mean to tell me, just to receive a big payday. I have to spend seventy-five percent of my life on a job until I'm old enough to cash out my 401k? That's hell on earth if you ask me.

Growing up as a kid, I had both my biological father and my step father in my life. Neither one of them told me the workforce in the world would be as hard as this.

For the first ten years of my life, I watched my real father work from sunrise to sunset cutting cane by hand with a machete. He would come home drenched in sweat from a long hot day under the sun. To make matters worse, he was required to wear long sleeves because of the chemicals from the cane, that didn't help regardless. My sister and I never bothered asking for piggy back rides after he got off work because we knew he was exhausted.

He worked such hard labor that payday didn't even put a smile on his face. He said his check didn't add up despite all of the hard labor that was done.

I couldn't understand why my father was always broke and all he ever did was work. He never had any bad habits, and I don't think he was bad with managing money or had a secret family he was taking care of. Come to find out, the company he was working for didn't want to increase his income and that's what kept him broke. Eleven dollars an hour can't take care of a house dog. So what was it supposed to do for a family of four? That's right, not much.

Although, my father's body may have been beat up. When it came down to work he would never miss, because he knew if he missed one day of working less than ten hours a day, we would've been living in poverty.

Sometimes my father would weep out about Mr. Paul, not giving any raises out, my mother would suggest that he quit, but he was in fear of falling behind in bills. Besides he was limited to other jobs because companies weren't hiring in the area like that even though they kept a 'help wanted' sign in the window.

This made my father job scared and comfortable with relying on a check, which led to unhappiness. But he wasn't the only one unhappy in his place of work.

For example, my stepfather had a good job. I mean benefits, insurance for the family, retirement, and he made twenty-five dollars an hour plus overtime doing the same work my father was doing but instead, he used a machine for another company. And unlike my real father, he would get a yearly raise during the holiday season. My stepfather was paid! I mean with a Capital "P".

However, with all the money he was making. He was just as unhappy with his job as my real father. In the thirty years of working for the same company, he dealt with being picked on because of his Jamaican accent, being treated like an outcast, and management overlooking his credentials to be a supervisor just so they can pass down supervisor jobs to their family members. I thought the same thing you are probably thinking now.

Why should it matter if he got a supervisor position? At least he's getting paid, that's all that should matter. But my stepfather wasn't regular, he cared about the people and he wanted a supervisor position to empower the people and increase the value of the company.

He though, if he could just hold a high position in a well-paying company that he could make changes and ensure nobody got mistreated like him.

I learned a few things from my both fathers work experience; don't allow myself to get comfortable on this pallet jack, acknowledge my worth, and never allow a job that I'm not comfortable working to hold me back.

In my humble opinion all of our time is way more valuable than eleven dollars an hour or to accept mistreatment. Yes I do understand that you need to have a stepping stone in life to get where you're trying to go, but don't get comfortable staying at level one. Use that eleven dollar job as experience because if you don't, fear will always control you. Think about it, anytime you have a great idea or plan you want to put action behind, fear creeps in and tries to stop you from being great. Right?

And after witnessing my both fathers work history, and the fear they both experienced, I refuse to let any job put fear in me. No company will ever control me with a dollar or a position because we are living in a time that I can create my own wealth and lifestyle. I get it, it's not gonna be easy, but it's attainable and I rather chase that than to chase a biweekly check or position.

Addressing The Congregation
By: Pastor Elder Blaze
(The community pastor)

"Amen church!

I said Amen church!

First off, let's thank God for his wonderful divine spirit that watches over each and every one of us.

Second, I would like to thank you all for making it to the house of the Lord this morning. With the heavy rain outside, I didn't think we would be able to have church. But since we're all here; church we shall have."

(The congregation clapped their hands and praised God).

Pastor Elder Blaze added. "That's right church, praise Him, because he is mighty and worthy of all praise. Although Pastor Blaze stood at the altar with a smile on his face, he was bothered when he saw a young lady going through the trash cans in the back of church."

"Church!" Pastor Blaze called out into the microphone while holding his Bible up to be seen. The congregation quieted down and gave the Pastor their full undivided attention. Pastor Blaze removed his glasses with his free hand and wiped the sweat from his forehead and stuffed his handkerchief back into his jacket pocket.

"It's been brought to my attention by the Lord himself that we aren't living according to his word. In Matthew Chapter 22 verse 39, The Bible says: Thou shalt love thy neighbor as thyself." Before Pastor Blaze went any further with his message, he calmly stepped down from the podium to get eye level with the members of the church. Before saying another word, he raised the Bible again and said,

"Are we living in accordance with God's word? Do we really love our neighbors as thyself or are we just pretending as if God can't see right through to our heart?"

All of a sudden, the church got quiet. Instead of feeling the presence of the lord, you could feel the presence of embarrassment, fear, and all the hidden secrets the members of the congregation have been keeping to themselves.

However, that wasn't Pastor Blaze's concern. He was more concerned about Shantae roaming through the trash out back.

"Church, how blind could we be to not see one of God's creations in need of our help? We all should be ashamed. God has placed a beautiful soul around the church and we overlooked it because we are all too busy with our own life to see the message written on the wall. Our young sister Shantae has been

Going through our trash for months looking for any scraps of food that can get her and her kids through the day. We have not done our part in loving thy neighbor. None of us here knows what it feels like to be homeless and I'm sure none of us here wants to be homeless. But to overlook someone who needs us is ungodly and we need to repent today. Let's right our wrong, and not think or see ourselves better than anyone else. God told us to be there for one another. Not only for the ones gathered here at church, but for the entire human race. Amen?"

Amen! The church replied and the pastor ended service on that note. You can tell Pastor's message had gotten through to the members. They all formed a circle after service and began discussing ways to build and help the homeless in the community, starting with Shantae.

Power
By: Mayor Vereen
(The Evil Corrupted Mayor)

"Mayor Vereen, is everything okay?" Secretary Stacy asked.

"No, not quite." Mayor Vereen said.

"Ms. Betty- Ann ambushed me in my office, and said I don't know what's best for the people in the glades community. How dare she? I was born and raised right here in Belle Glade. I may not know much about MLK Boulevard, but I am confident in knowing what my people need to advance."

Although Mayor Vereen was pissed at Betty-Ann, he was more pissed at security for allowing her into the building. When he called for security to remove her they were a little too late, Betty-Ann had already given the Mayor a mouth full to destroy his ego.

After everything calmed down and Ms. Betty- Ann was escorted out, Mayor Vereen went into his office and closed the door. He sat in his big comfortable patriotic chair behind his desk, and stared at the American flag that was hanging in the corner of the office near all the great books he had read during his college days.

"Who have I become?" The Mayor asked himself.

"I am the one person in power that can help change the community, and give my people a better opportunity. But here I am, doing the same as my Colleagues that work in the state capital. Robbing my people from Government funds, youth centers, and nursing homes. And for what? A vacation home that I only visit two weeks out of the year? Or have expensive dinners with people I don't like? Or maybe I'm just stealing to challenge myself on how much government money I can stack into my bank account before getting caught and thrown into jail." The Mayor was sweating through his suit as began to grow scared and nervous of his greed. He kept replaying over and over in his head what Ms. Betty-Ann said to him.

"Son, I have been to many funerals during my life on this earth and not one time have I seen a U-Haul driving behind a Hurst."

Community Outreach
By: Sister Elaina
(Youth leader)

"Excuse me, Excuse me." I said as I approached a woman walking with two kids. "Sorry to bother you ma'am, but I just wanted to hand you a flyer for the First Community Baptist Church of God located on Martin Luther King boulevard in the old Afro Supremes building.

If you are not busy this Saturday, come by and check us out. We'll be giving away free food, clothes, and toys for the kids.

All activities this summer are funded through the Dominique Foundation (an NFL player) so if you decide to sign your kids up, there will be no fees included.

If I can be honest ma'am, this would be a great opportunity that you and your kids can benefit from. At the First Community Baptist Church of God, we're similar to the Boys & Girls Club. We not only let your kids play here, we instill them with valuable life lessons as well. For example, one thing that we always teach our students is; 'your health is your most valuable asset.' Most of all, we teach them the importance of having God in their lives. We have a really good program here ma'am, and it would be nice to see you stop by. Thank you so much for your time!"

Credit
By: Kimberly Blackmon
(Single mother with bad credit)

"Shaniqua, girl please!!! You don't see me doing something?

My God!

Every time I'm taking care of business you start aggravating me. If you're hungry, you know how to fix your own food. But, make sure you wash your hands before you dig into my pots, and don't use my China plates either. There's paper plates and plastic silverware in the pantry, I'm not trying to wash any dishes. Between you and the credit bureau I'm not sure who is more aggravating.

This is my fourth time on the phone with them this week, and yet still, my credit score is below five hundred. I paid them what was owed, and still there's no increase on my credit score. What really gets under my skin is, they don't have an answer as to why my score hasn't increased.

All they ever say is "we're working on it Ms. Blackmon". Which is not cool with me, when they called for me to pay my debt, I paid them. I didn't hesitate to give up the $1,500. I may have cried about it, but I gave it up. All I know is, today there better be an increase to my credit or I'm emailing their headquarters as soon as I get off the phone.

## Drunk
### By: Mr. Earl Roosevelt
### (Unstable)

"Mr. Roosevelt I can't allow you to keep coming on the jobsite drunk. It'll be a big lawsuit for the company if you get hurt and then I gotta hear it from my father. Look at you; you can barely stand on your own two feet. I'm sorry but I can't let you work under these conditions.

I'll call Danny to get you a ride home so you can sleep it off. Normally I would write you up but you have been working for my dad so many years, this would break his heart. Seeing his favorite employee, drunk in a place of business. He really believes in you and thinks you qualify to run this entire department.

But if you keep coming to work hungover you may not get the opportunity. Please Earl no more; I would hate to be the guy to tell my dad that you don't deserve the opportunity to be supervisor over the shipping department. Go home and get some rest, I'll see you first thing in the morning."

Serve God or Else
By: Pastor Elder Blaze
(First Sunday)

"Church...!" Pastor Elder Blaze said.
"I said Church!!!" He repeated in the microphone. "We have a full house here today; I see the lord has spoken to many this early Sunday morning. That shows he's working this morning. I don't think y'all heard me though." Pastor Blaze said before repeating himself.

"I said we have a full house here early this morning, the good Lord is working!!" Pastor Blaze took a drink of water from his glass before opening his Bible. But after looking over the crowd of church members, he closed his Bible.

"Today, I had in mind to preach from John chapter 3 verse 16 but God has laid something else on my heart that I want to talk to y'all about, is that okay?" The church members replied, "It's okay with us Pastor." "Okay, right on." Pastor added.

"You know I was home Saturday afternoon sitting on my back porch and I thought to myself, if I don't serve or believe in God who else do I have?" It was quiet in the church. You can tell everyone that was listening suddenly asked themselves the same question that Pastor asked himself Saturday. Nobody had an answer. Pastor immediately smiled at the people. That's right!!! Jesus is all we have and we must trust and believe in him, because without him we don't have anyone who will step in and die on behalf of our sins, anger, lust, lies and whatever else we choose over him.

## Car Wash
### By: Shaniqua
### (The girl that understands)

"Mom, can you take me downtown to Adrian's car wash? Please! I have to be there before 8." Shaniqua said while brushing her teeth.

"Adrian's car wash? Shaniqua girl, why do you need to go to Adrian's car wash before 8?"

"It's my first day of work. He hired me to pick up the trash around the building. Oh, and don't worry he pays me under the table, so when it's time to file taxes you can still be able to file me as a dependent." Shaniqua said while putting on her tennis shoes with the hole on the side.

"I figured since your job hasn't called you to come back to work, the least I could do is help out from the little bit of cash I'll be making at the car wash on Saturday's and Sunday's. You know mom I'm not letting you stop me from carrying my weight around here. I may be young but I am smart enough to know when we are struggling and I know that every bit of help counts. Besides, your job might be calling back any day now and all the money I make from picking up trash can go towards my dance classes." Shaniqua's mom Kimberly just looked at her because she couldn't say anything. She knew her daughter wasn't taking no for an answer, so she grabbed the keys off the table and told Shaniqua to meet her in the car.

## Selfish
By: Mayor Vereen
(Money hungry)

"Stacy, I don't give a damn. I don't care who lives in that apartment complex, they all need to be moved out by the first of next month. I have plans for this property and affordable living is not one of them. I need that building knocked down by this summer so the contractor can start working on my next luxury apartments."

"But Mr. Mayor, these apartments are historic! When African Americans were freed from slavery, that complex was the first place they all migrated to form Unity amongst themselves." Secretary Stacy said.

"I don't give a damn, I said what I said. I want that building gone by the end of the month. If I have to forcefully move them out, I will. I'm the mayor, I can have all utilities cut and what choice would they be left with then?" Mr. Vereen didn't care that eighty percent of the residents were elders and twenty percent were single parents which was the real reason the rent was affordable. This guy was so money hungry that he was willing to do anything to add more zeros to his bank account. Even if that meant being a crab in a barrel and throwing others down to step on their necks. It was written in the Bible (Acts chapter 20 verse 35) that "It is more blessed to give than to receive."

But that's something the Mayor wouldn't understand. He wouldn't understand that he could find more joy in giving with a pure heart than taking for selfish gain. You could tell something has triggered the Mayor to get him to this point, but that's something he has to share with someone more qualified, which is the good Lord.

## Baby Daddy
### By: Teresa (B.J older sister)
### (Conversation with bestfriend)

"Chelsea girl! Let me tell you what my baby daddy Alvin said. So, I called him the other night to ask for money for our son, because little Alvin needed more school clothes right. Alvin already knows that I just paid $600 to get my car out the shop, so I figured he wouldn't mind helping out to get our son clothes.

Girl tell me why he thought that I was scamming him because it was his pay week. He answered the phone talkin' bout, "what you want Teresa? Every time it's pay day your number shows up on my phone. Just last week I sent you money, what could Junior (little Alvin) possibly need now?"

So I told him little Alvin outgrew his clothes, and I needed help to get him more. This fool had the nerve to say 'it's not his problem and he bought Junior clothes at the beginning of the school year.' Girl! You know I had to lay him straight!

I let him know that the $200 he sends Junior every OTHER MONTH is only enough to cover his after school activities which isn't really satisfying what the courts would've made him pay if I put him on child support. Girl! I was so upset with him. I can't tell you the last time he saw his son and he's always trying to flirt his way back into my life. I'll tell you this, if he doesn't want to give me the money, I'll be the first person in line next Monday to let the judge know Alvin King needs to be on child support. I am tired of our son being punished, for his father's irresponsibility."

Visitors
By:Darrell Woodson & Julian Baker
(Student athlete vs. Normal student)

(Darrell)

Dad, The University of Florida wants to visit us this Friday at home. So please don't forget to take off from work that day.

It's going to be an hour visit, they just want to talk with you and me, get to know us and try to force me into sign my scholarship with them early. I told them I'm still leaving my options open until signing day (the day that athletes have to sign their scholarships). Once that question comes up we will flip the conversation and start asking them questions about their academic programs, student dormitory and the safety of students on campus.

Although I love the University of Florida dad, I really just want to pick the right school to further my education because what if baseball doesn't work out? At least I will have a degree to fall back on. By the way, I wanna thank you for allowing me to make my own decision and not pressuring me into what you think is best for me. I love you for being supportive.

(Julian)

Mom, Harvard University Academic program wants to stop by and congratulate me on being one of the top students in the nation to receive their most prestigious scholarship. Please be home in time for our visitors. I don't want to have them waiting because it won't be a good look. I wrote down some programs I would like to ask them about.

For example, their Technology program, entrepreneurship, innovation program, leadership and management program. I'm telling you mama some of the billionaires of the world today went to school there. This school is one of the best elite institutions on this planet.

I know I know mama, that's not saying I will become a billionaire because billionaires attended school there. But let's just say, I will work my butt off to become successful just like the billionaire alumni of Harvard University. You taught me the meaning of working hard that's why those visitors are showing up at our front door.

Community Fish Fry
By: The Community
(Good Energy)

Let us pray this day never comes to an end. Look how happy and powerful we are when we spread unconditional love. The young assisting the old, the adults instructing the teens, and the kids just simply being kids. The Lord is smiling down on us today.

Not once did I hear a negative comment or an argument all day, I only saw hugs and kisses. This day is one for the books. Although the sun is going down behind the trees, smiles of happiness are keeping the sky from going dark. This is the way it should be, not just today but every day.

Recap
By: Betty-Ann
(Well respected elder)

My God, I never thought I'd see the day you would show your face. Can't nobody in the community tell me that you weren't amongst the people at yesterday's fish fry. Although you don't care much for the music and alcohol, you still found a way to fellowship with the crowd by communicating through laughter, and eating fish.

Yes, I might have been the only one that saw you because of my relationship with you, but I guarantee every individual felt your presence. I waited years for you to clean this community and get rid of all its demons. Now that your hands have touched this place I can die in peace because you've got it from here.

The Storm Before The Calm
By:The community
(In Fear of the weather)

It was 12:00 in the afternoon and the sky was pitch dark. If you didn't have a flashlight or a cellphone light on it was hard to get around because the street lights were out. The wind was up to 10 miles per hour and started to pick up at the speed of light. The clouds were singing loud scares of thunder that were followed by raindrops the size of small stones.

Everyone in the community was frightened by what was taking place and there was no time to board up windows, fill up our gas tanks, or buy food. Everyone just ran inside and watched from the window. For thirty long minutes, a massive storm took over our poverty-stricken community. The rain came down like an endless waterfall, and the wind blew so viscously it shook our windows. We were afraid it would never end.

After the storm was over, the whole community came out to see the damages that were done. Windows were broken and outdoor furniture was blown away, but thankfully nobody was killed or hurt during this storm. As we assessed the damage, we couldn't help but notice how bright the sky had become. It was like the storm came to clean our community and give us a fresh start. We all felt the positive energy and wanted more of that in our community.

## Curious
## By: Brother Nelson
## (God's Ability)

"Mr. Nelson, you remember me?

Last week, when you were talking to the fellas about God down at the church you attend, I was one of those kids. I know it seems like we weren't listening, and were teasing you about your dress code, but not me, I had tunnel vision and I was eager to know more about God's love, care and forgiveness."

"I don't mind telling you how wonderful God is, he's worthy to be praised, son. I remember when I was a youngster just like you, but I was much more foolish and immature. You are nearly years ahead of me, because when I was your age, I didn't care to know God. I mean, I was so hellish and stuck in my ways nobody wanted to help me. I would go to school and pick fights with other kids, and as for the nerdy kids... Well, I mean the smart kids.

They didn't have a chance surviving my torture. Anything they valued I destroyed or it was mine by the end of the day. I turned eighteen and was still in the 10th grade so I decided to stop going to school. When you don't have the education to get a job, the streets are the place you go to look for work or anything you're missing in your life because they embrace you before anybody else. You know why? Because they don't want to lose by themselves. They want to take someone down with them, so they give you a shoulder to lean on. That's what this older guy by the name of Rabbit-toe did for me, he embraced me like a little brother and I started selling drugs

51

for him. I would run the eastern side of Belle Glade while he had this white kid by the name of Marley at the northern end of Belle Glade. Us three were getting money, or at least that's what I thought. Once Rabbit-toe made what he thought was enough, he took the money and skipped town, because the feds (Federal law enforcers) were in town to arrest all drug dealers. He was eventually caught on other charges.

However, Marley and I were so young and unaware of how things go, after he left we got caught selling drugs to a federal law enforcer. I'm talking about a backpack filled with all different drugs, and we both were facing a life sentence without a chance of parole.

While on trial, my mother would come visit me everyday up until her last day on earth. She ended up dying while I was facing life. So in place of her, Pastor Elder Blaze would come pray for me and read me Bible verses. He told me, "Son, if you just believe in the high power of God he'll set you free from the hold the Devil has on you."

"Me being who I am, I didn't have time to worry about God or wait on him. I was too busy worrying about being convicted. Nevertheless, one day I was waiting on Pastor Elder Blaze to come see me and he didn't show. So I went back to my bump (bed) and I laid there. I noticed I didn't have any options to win my case so why not try this wonderful God out. Now I can say he's the reason I'm able to stand here today and share how wonderful he is. I did three years in prison and was released. With the power of God, He made it possible that I didn't spend my entire life in prison."

Curious
By: Brother Nelson
(God's Ability)

"Mr. Nelson, you remember me?

Last week, when you were talking to the fellas about God down at the church you attend, I was one of those kids. I know it seems like we weren't listening, and were teasing you about your dress code, but not me, I had tunnel vision and I was eager to know more about God's love, care and forgiveness."

"I don't mind telling you how wonderful God is, he's worthy to be praised, son. I remember when I was a youngster just like you, but I was much more foolish and immature. You are nearly years ahead of me, because when I was your age, I didn't care to know God. I mean, I was so hellish and stuck in my ways nobody wanted to help me. I would go to school and pick fights with other kids, and as for the nerdy kids... Well, I mean the smart kids.

They didn't have a chance surviving my torture. Anything they valued I destroyed or it was mine by the end of the day. I had turned eighteen and was still in the 10th grade so I decided to stop going to school. When you don't have the education to get a job, the streets are the place you go to look for work or anything you're missing in your life because they embrace you before anybody else. You know why? Because they don't want to lose by themselves. They want to take someone down with them, so they give you a shoulder to lean on. That's what this older guy by the name of Rabbit-toe did for me, he embraced me like a little brother and I started selling drugs

53

for him. I would run the eastern side of Belle Glade while he had this white kid by the name of Marley at the northern end of Belle Glade. Us three were getting money, or at least that's what I thought. Once Rabbit-toe made what he thought was enough, he took the money and skipped town,

because the feds (Federal law enforcers) were in town to arrest all drug dealers. He was eventually caught on other charges.

However, Marley and I were so young and unaware of how things go, after he left we got caught selling drugs to a federal law enforcer. I'm talking about a backpack filled with all different drugs, and we both were facing a life sentence without a chance of parole. While on trial, my mother would come visit me everyday up until her last day on earth. She ended up dying while I was facing life. So in place of her, Pastor Elder Blaze would come pray for me and read me Bible verses. He told me, "Son, if you just believe in the high power of God he'll set you free from the hold the Devil has on you."

"Me being who I am, I didn't have time to worry about God or wait on him. I was too busy worrying about being convicted.

Nevertheless, one day I was waiting on Pastor Elder Blaze to come see me and he didn't show. So I went back to my bump (bed) and I laid there. I noticed I didn't have any options to win my case so why not try this wonderful God out. Now I can say he's the reason I'm able to stand here today and share how wonderful he is. I did three years in prison and was released. With the power of God, He made it possible that I didn't spend my entire life in prison."

# Our Community

This Is It
By: Betty-Ann
(Heaven earthly angle)

Excuse me nurse, today can you not open the blinds to my room. I want to keep as much sunlight out as possible. Today is just one of those days. Oh, and could you hold off on the visitors for the day?

I just want to spend some time alone and lay here in peace. Thank you so much! Another thing sweetheart, do you mind closing the door behind you? Thank you. I appreciate it!

(Door closes)

Okay, God.

It's just you and I in here and I know you've come to take back your soul, but before you do I want to thank you so much for allowing me to live a long prosperous life.

I have lived longer than some of my kids, and it's only right for it to be my time to go. Although I'm not sure what death brings, I understand that everyone's days are numbered on this earth.

I couldn't be more excited to come be with you. Deep down in my heart, I know I did as your word (the Bible) commanded me to do. Loved my neighbor as I loved myself, obeyed your commands, and praised your name, I did it all by your amazing grace. Oh, lord how I am so impatient to see heaven. Come do as you came to do, and again thank you for your amazing love and grace.

Self-conscious
By: Mayor Vereen
(Self conscious)

I feel that something is missing, but I have no clue what it could be. I am the mayor of the city, my newest project is in the making and I have a beautiful family. Yet still I feel like a part of my soul has vanished away. I've worked my whole entire life for this moment and yet still, I'm not happy.

Honestly, I can't be that oblivious to think I feel like this for no reason. I have done so much evil that my whole life purely runs off of my wrongful ways. I don't have a generous bone in my body, I am selfish, controlling, and manipulating.

Sadly, I don't know where to stop, and I'm not sure if I want to stop either. But I know I have a decision to make before I walk out of this office of mines. Do I give this all up and do my first work over with God? Or do I continue to be this evil maniac that lives the life of a liar and will be put to shame when God pulls back the curtain?

## I Am Not That
## By: BJ
(Reckless by association)
(I'm not who you think I am)

I don't have an appointment, but I'm here to see Officer Webster. He's not expecting me or anything, I just have a problem and he's a well-known officer in the community so I thought he could help.

"Okay, no problem, what's your name sir? So I can tell him that you're out here looking for him."

My name is Blake Johnson but he might know me by B.J; Jay murk's little cousin.

"Okay, sit tight and I'll let him know you're out here in the lobby."

"Thank you sir!"

"Hey, what's going on B.J?" Officer Webster said coming out from the double doors.

"Nothing, I just wanted to stop by because I have a dilemma. I don't want to waste your time so let me jump right into it. You know Officer Webster, seeing my family being dismantled by my Cousin Jay Murk's death really made me take a step back and view my life.

I know you and the entire force see my family as a menace to the society because of the crimes my cousin has committed, but in all honesty Mr. Webster, I've never committed any crime. Not with my cousin, not by myself and that's why I am here. I spent a lot of time with Jay Murk and it put a huge spotlight on me for the things I don't display.

It makes me uncomfortable knowing that people see me for something I'm not. Saying things like 'this stupid ignorant black kid doesn't know any better and eventually he'll do just like the rest and end up in jail.'

I'm actually a good kid filled with dreams and aspirations of becoming wealthy to help my family just like any other black man or black woman around here.

.

Rehabilitation
By: Mr. Earl Roosevelt
(City worker)
(Alcoholic)

"Hey Jake, I really appreciate you not telling your father about my incident the other day. I understand that you guys are running a well-oiled machine around here and you guys can't afford some airhead like me to screw that up. That's why I decided to take a leave of absence from work, and check myself into a rehabilitation center for drunks to deal with my alcohol addiction. I am tired and too old to be killing myself with toxic liquid.

There were times I wasn't sure who the guy was in the mirror because one minute I would be fine and the next I would be depressed, angry and ready to hurt anyone in my path. It's scary knowing that you have no control over your own behavior. If it wasn't for my wife taking money out of our account for the bills, I know for a fact we would have gone without lights and water. It's embarrassing to even tell you this, but at least I was able to come to terms with myself and find help. I'm not sure how I got to this point and I'm not sure how long I'll be in there, but I just ask that you guys hold my position while I'm gone."

Elite Women
By: Sister Elaina
(Ladies Empowerment Meeting)

"Girls ages 15 and older please stay behind, I would like to have a word with you. The rest of the youth group is dismissed. We will pick up where we left off next time but make sure y'all call all the parents before leaving out of the church. Thank you and I'll see y'all next week.

As for you young ladies here, I can't express enough gratitude towards you beautiful princesses. I am so proud of each and every one of you. I've watched you guys grow, mature and become leaders for the younger girls.

All credit goes to Jesus Christ, because he is the source behind this unbreakable sisterhood.

Not to put you on the spot but look at you Mimi. Three months ago you would always come in here with an attitude when your mother would drop you off. Now it's impossible for me to stop you from smiling. And as for you Jocelyn, my God, girl you were a hand-full to deal with.

Your mother would call me in the middle of the night crying and telling me how you would sneak out the house and wouldn't come home until morning. Now she shares stories of you never wanting to leave the house, only focusing on your schoolwork and wanting to become a surgeon.

Like I told you ladies before, with the help of God and prayer anything is possible. I pray for you ladies every day and I want you all to know I love y'all and I am here for you no matter what. If God changed me I know he can do the same for you.

Clueless
By: William Williamson
(Clueless Community Mentor)

How could I not see the answers that were so obviously placed in front of me? These kids are constantly in survival mode. At home they go nights without food and at school they're getting bullied for wearing Walmart shoes. That's a whole lot to take on as a child and it has caused them to act out. See, our community lacks the resources and funds to create recreational centers and after school programs to keep our children out of trouble. The parents of our community have tried endlessly to raise money but the plan always fails because they are overworked and underpaid.

It saddens me to see what this community has become because for over a decade I served as a community mentor and I want things to be how they once were. By a thread of a needle this country town is barely holding on to what's left. For years I couldn't figure out why my heart wouldn't allow me to leave Belle Glade, but I now realize that God kept me here to restore this community back to its rightful place. I have decided that I will be the voice for this community. I will make the calls to the city council, the governor, and a couple of friends that are able to put up the finances for a foundation. When Monday comes I will call around first thing to get the process started.

Do it for me
By: Harry Pete
(Bragging about my friend)

Darrell, my boy, my best friend, the legendary baseball player. How's it going my brother? I hope all is well. I just stopped by to check on my extended family.Darrell, we have been friends since we could remember right? We played in sandboxes together, shared birthday parties, and took tub baths together. We have done mostly everything together my brother, we are inseparable. Through all the years of knowing each other, I have never asked you for anything.But today that changes cuz' Ima need a favor from you my boy. Tomorrow night against your rival team, Ima need you to hit a homerun. Knock that shit out of the stadium.

Yesterday, I was over near Malcolm community park shooting hoops and me and some other dudes got into an argument about who's the greatest baseball player to ever come from Belle Glade. Of course, I said you because what you are doing has never been done in the history of high school baseball, 34 Home Runs, a batting average of 300 and player of the year as a junior, I mean the stats speak for themselves. They didn't agree but you know how it goes, haters gonna hate. Right after I shared your stats, that's when they started to heavily express that you weren't that good. They said sports news and your supporters hype you up because of your likable image. They also said, all your big games were played against spoiled amateur brats who've never really competed. But I beg to differ, I told them about all the hard, stressful nights when you refused to leave the field until you got your swing perfect, and the days you would spend an entire Saturday hitting fast balls or fielding ground balls. I really wanted them to understand this moment of being celebrated, didn't come easy, you worked your ass off for this. I know because you've dragged me out to the field most of those nights.

So if you could, please hit a home run so I can tell them I told you so. And if you're feeling good, hit two home runs. I love you man, I believe in you, and it's no secret that you're well on your way to the league. When you make it don't forget about your loved ones. We all believe in you Darrell, make this community proud.

Credit Bureau/Let Me Help You
By: Kimberly Blackmon
(Credit bureau conversation)

"Ms. Blackmon are you still there?

Okay, thank you for holding.

Now let's see; As I was looking through your files. I came across an issue that may answer why your credit score hasn't increased.

Do you know a male by the name of Perry Hollis? Right here we have him listed as your husband. He's the reason why your credit score is being held captive. He has two car payments under your name, and a recent loan for a condo, thats pending towards your credit.

Ms. Blackmon, I don't want to speak out of terms here. But, this seems a little sketchy to me. On paper Mr. Hollis is listed as your husband. I can see that you guys don't share the same last name or address, but your signature has been signed off on everything that was purchased on your credit card. This brings me to the conclusion that maybe your identity is being used without your knowledge and your signature is being forged on paper.

I'm not sure who Mr. Hollis is to you or if you even know this guy, but he has access to your identity and all of your personal information. I'm not supposed to tell you, but he also has bank accounts open in your name with his name added on the account. I understand you're horrified, I can tell by the sound of your voice that you are surprised.

So this is what I'm going to do for you, I am going to

waive all transactions made against your credit in the last 6 months. That way your credit score will go up a hundred points, and that will put you in the average range.

Oh no, don't thank me.

Thank God, it's him that made me realize how important it is to pull others up by the hand. We all need some kind of assistance in life, and if I can be a help to someone why not? Just promise me that you won't stop fighting to improve your credit. Credit is extremely important in today's time. The better your credit, the bigger your loan will be for that business you've wanted to start or that dream home you always wanted to buy.

I'm sure, I don't have to lecture you on credit. Obviously you know what it means in today's world, and that's why you are calling. I know you're on the right track and I can't wait to hear from you in a couple months, I expect your score to be above average. Is there anything else I can do for today?

Okay, thank you and have a blessed day.

Funeral
By: The community
(Immortal)

Our hearts cry in sorrow because we will never see her again. O'lord how I pray that we cherish the lessons and wisdom Betty-Ann has left behind. Every individual in here today was lucky enough to witness the angelic soul of this beautiful elderly lady. Whether it was getting on our tails for something we did wrong. Or congratulating us with kisses on the cheek and hugs tighter than the grip of pliers, we took something so precious for granted and disposed of it alongside the city trash.Although our hearts are heavy saying goodbye to our beloved Betty-Ann, let's not forget the memories and valuable lessons she gave us. May her spirit live within us all.

In memory of our beloved Betty-Ann

Health or addiction?
By: Mr. Earl Roosevelt
(Rehab treatment)

Oh how good it feels to be free as a bird. Going to a rehab really helped me realize that there's more to life than drinking alcohol. I have a lovely wife, amazing kids, and beautiful grandkids that need me around as long as possible.

While in rehab I learned how having a drinking addiction causes the body to break down. It can cause kidney failure, liver damage, cancer and a lot other diseases that will eventually move your expiration date closer. Thank God when I was tested I didn't have any health issues.

However, I can't say the same for some of the others I met in my AA meeting. I met a guy by the name of Glaze, he was a really nice fella but he had major health problems. He was surviving off of one kidney and a liver that could collapse at any moment. The guy was a walking miracle. During my time of treatment, I saw him struggling just to lift himself out of a chair and that scared me. I don't want to deal with kidney failure or liver damage and I sure as hell wasn't ready to die. I chose my health over alcohol and it was the best decision I've ever made.

As for my rehab buddy Glaze, he wasn't given the chance to fight his addiction one more time. He ended up dying in his sleep due to kidney failure. Blood had got into his lung and somehow affected his kidney. Over his dead body, I promise him that I wouldn't take another drink out of respect for his soul. I haven't even thought about drinking since being released from rehab.

## Championship
## By: Darrell Woodson
## (Bottom of the 9th)

Bottom of the 9th with two outs and I am up to bat. The bases are loaded, and we are down by one point. With two strikes, I have to be very careful and watch out for the curveball.

I gripped my bat tight and thought to myself "This is the moment I've been waiting for, the win that will make us three times champions." I stepped back into the batter box, and began to zone in on every sudden move the pitcher made. He wined up his arm and I said to myself "okay, here we go Darrell, a fastball coming directly down the middle." Before I can set my feet to swing.

Poof!

The ball slammed right into the catcher's mit.

"Strike three you're out!" The umpire said.

A curveball, just like I thought it would be. I wasn't even close to slamming the pitch out of the park in fact I missed the ball by a hundred feet.

I was so broken; I hung my head and walked back to the dugout.

What will everyone say? I let the entire community down, the fans, coaches, alumni's, and most important my homie Harry Pete who bet money that I would hit a homerun. This can't be true I thought to myself, how a five star baseball player strikes out in a time like this.

As I was packing all of my equipment into my bag,

Harry, who was bragging all game about me, walked into the dugout. "My boy, I know you are not dwelling on that strike out. I understand you're hurt because you guys didn't get the chance to make history three times in a row. But look on the bright side, you got the opportunity to finish your senior season playing in a championship game when other schools didn't even make it this far.

Hold your up head homie, you're blessed, there's teenagers around the world who would die to be in your shoes. You have a full ride scholarship, and maybe even a chance to play in the major league which is very dope. So don't sit around drowning in sorrow because in the game of sports, you lose some, and you win some."

Harry is going to make a great encouraging father one day. He was right, not every game will be a win or I will play at my fullest potential. What matters is, I keep my head up and continue to give my all and that's with everything I do in life.

God's On Time
By:Shaniqua Blackmon
(Thankful)

Dear God,

Hmm...Let me see... I'm not sure where to start this prayer because we haven't spoken in a while. I've been super busy trying to help my mother by supporting myself financially.

Bills are drowning her, and she hasn't received any calls for a job opportunity. Right when things couldn't have gotten any worse, you stepped right in and blessed her.

After the credit bureau decided they were not going to help out mama, she received a call with a job opportunity, that she didn't have to interview for. Things are on the rise for us and I know you played an important role in our upcoming blessings.

I don't know how to thank you because I am ashamed for not trusting that you would show up on time. But, I guess I can say that praying right now is a form of thanking you.

Thank you for life, everlasting love, and blessings that we sometimes don't deserve. As humans we get in the way of your work by believing in our own power versus your mighty hands.

I'll be the first to say we don't mean anything by it. We're just afraid of the unknown, afraid of failure, and being uncomfortable.

But thanks to you, being uncomfortable and afraid will never swallow us because you know when to come to our rescue.

## The Bible says:

Do not fear, for I am with you; do not be afraid, for I am your God. I will strengthen you; I will help you; I will hold on to you with my righteous right hand.
–Isaiah chapter 41 verse 10

During my short life on this earth, I saw no lie in your word. Once again, thank you!


Amen!

Unsure
By: BJ
(Confused kid)

Dear Heavenly Father,

As I kneel before you in prayer, I must tell you that I am confused. I have no clue how to live the life of a good disciple and show my appreciation for you dying on the cross for our sins.

I never was taught what I am allowed and not allowed to do. The most I was ever taught was to protect myself and don't answer any questions the police ask. I can't lie, being a sinner was so much easier than living for you. Every time I want to do well, I sin and I over think what punishment I will be receiving.

When I had no knowledge of you, I saw no wrong in the way I was living. My response to everything was always "it is what it is", or "that's just life". Which never made me wanna pull my hair out my head. Then again, I am confused because there are times you have covered me with your merciful hands.

For example, the same day my cousin lost his life, I was supposed to be with him. But you put your hedge of protection over me.

Lord the words of what I'm really trying to say is not coming out. I mean, I guess what I'm really saying is that I don't know how to live for you quite yet as my Lord and savior. It's something new to me and it's gonna take some time getting used to what I can and can't do. So I ask that you please be patient with me as I try my best to change from my terrible habits.

Amen

Texting Buddy
By: Teresa (BJ older sister)
(Speaking truly from the heart)

Hey Bernard,

Thanks for dinner tonight, it was amazing and the food was delicious. I never knew we had a gourmet restaurant in town, which goes to show how much I pay attention to my surroundings.

LOL (Laughing Out loud)

However, I do have something I would like to share with you. During dinner tonight, you asked me if I was single and I told you yes.

Although it's true, I'm really not looking to start dating again right now. Don't get me wrong, I did enjoy our dinner date and the deep conversations we've had, but the timing is off. Right now, I would love to just focus on myself and give myself more love before I start loving someone else again. I can't keep looking for guys to fill this empty space in my heart, I have to fill it myself. Besides that, I have dreams and goals I would like to accomplish in life. I wanna go back to school and maybe become a nurse practitioner so I can open up my own facility for the people right here in town. When I was younger, my grandmother would always tell me:

"God blesses those people who depend only on him. They belong to the kingdom of heaven!"

Matthew Chapter five verse three in the Bible, I still remember that verse from my childhood. Back then I didn't understand what my grandmother meant because I was too young, but now I know. I have grown up and tried my way at life and failed, but now I'm going to try God's way. I wanna start going back to church and eventually get baptized. My son and my soul are more important than any man could ever be, that's why I say I'm not ready to start dating again. I have to get my priorities in line and I don't need any distractions while doing so. I hope you understand where I am coming from, and I would like to remain friends if that's okay with you.

Message sent

Temptations
By: Brother Nelson
(Desperate)

Pastor, I come to you in a desperate time of need. Normally I can handle my own struggles but this time I need your help to assist me with my temptations. At my job we just hired a new female employee. A very well respected young lady around the same age as me. Last week Monday was her first day in the office and my manager Lucas asked me if I would be willing to train her.

I agreed to do so, because I was working on building my resume. I figured if I trained her, upper management would get a chance to see how knowledgeable and skillful I am with working with others. That way, there shouldn't be any excuses why I don't get the supervisor training position.

After being introduced we both sat behind my desk in the back of the office in a small cubic space. Pastor, the devil immediately attacked me. I never smelled a scent so good in my life. It's like her perfume manipulated me from everything I believed in. But it didn't stop there, every minute around the clock I would find myself sniffing the air around her. When she would ask questions pertaining to work, I would lose myself in watching the words roll off her lips.

It had gotten so bad at times I would catch myself watching her blouse hoping to see her cleavage, and that's what brought me here today, before I throw away everything I have and worked for I decided to reach out for help. I won't allow the devil to force me to sin against my wife.

**The Bible read:**

Husbands, love your wives, and do not be harsh with them.
-Colossians chapter 3 verse 19

As of right now pastor, I'm not loving my wife the way I should. I'm sinning against her love for me. That's why it was urgent for me to come see you. Let us pray this strong hold away from me.

**Praying...**

"Again I say to you, if two of you agree on earth about anything they ask, it will be done for them by my Father in heaven. For where two or three are gathered in my name, there am I among them."
-Matthew chapter 18 verse 19-20

Frenemies (Fake Friends)
By: Earl Roosevelt
(Dismiss)

Diana! Can you believe Bobby and fellas?

I went down to Paul's house to hang out with them like I do every Friday, and they started clowning me about my rehab visit and me not drinking anymore.

I took the insults like a man and laughed it off with them, but it really pissed me off when Abe tried to force me to take a drink knowing how bad off I was when I was drinking.

It's like he wanted to see me down bad again but I made a promise to myself that I was not going back to that state of mind. I worked extremely hard to get myself cleaned up, and for someone that I call a friend to try to get me into drinking again, is just shameful.

In fact none of them are no longer friends of mine. If they were real friends they would be congratulating me and encouraging my sobriety.

Although it hurts, I thank God for showing me who they truly are today. I realized that in order to maintain my sobriety, I must find friends who support my new lifestyle instead of tear it down. I am a new man and I can't have that kind of energy around me.

Guest Speaker
By: William Williamson (community mentor)
(The sky's the limit)

Royal Glades "Great Sharks" graduating class. Thank you for having me as a guest speaker at your most memorable ceremony.

You know I had a list of things that I wanted to talk about today, but after looking into the crowd and seeing all of these African American faces, I feel no need to have educational talk about staying out of trouble.

Instead, I need to congratulate each and every last one of you because this shows people that we are more than thugs, criminals, baby mommas, or baby daddies. We are the future, look to your right, now look to your left and tell each other "we are the future". One more time "we are the future".

That's right! Every one of you in a cap and gown today are special. You guys can be doctors, lawyers, judges, entertainers, and everything else you want to be. Sky's the limit. Yes, you will have hard times just like high school but don't give up and stop fighting until you reach your ultimate goal.

I am Mr. William Williamson, God bless and good luck on your journey in life.

When It's All Said And Done
By: Community
(God will have the last word)

As humans created by the hands of God, we tend to think we're all different. But we all share one thing in common, the urge to seek happiness.

Often times, we find ourselves stressed and pulling our hair out over small situations, but that's because we just want to be free of our problems and enjoy life as we dream it should be.

Nobody has the guide to this thing called "life" and to be honest I don't think it exists. We will always find ourselves stressed over things as small as what shirt to wear, or big things like the loss of a loved one. Stress knocks at the doorstep of every individual, and only God can free us of all the burdens lying upon our hearts.

God!!!
God!!! God!!! God!!! God!!!
Yes, God!!!

He has the mighty power to free our hearts and our minds of any captivity. We have to understand things may not look beautiful right away, but if we just trust that God has our back, any battle we face, we will always come out victorious.

Made in the USA
Las Vegas, NV
26 April 2021

22041960R00050